Diary of
Almost Co

Book 4

My New Buddy

Bill Campbell

Copyright © KC Global Enterprises Pty Ltd
All Rights Reserved

Friday

My eyes creep to the clock for the 20th time, still not lunchtime! Mrs. Snow White, our history teacher, obviously not her real name (unless I'm enrolled at Disney School) drones on and on and on....

I have a liking for giving the people in my life nicknames, I think it makes my life a bit more interesting. Her real name is Mrs. Tompkins but Snow White suits her so much more. Her hair is midnight black in color and straighter than my ruler. It falls in an unmoving mass down her back with a fake flower pinned to her head in case one crazy strand tries to get out of place. Her skin is white...not that - I don't go out much white...but more like Casper the Ghost white! Above her super intense blue eyes hang two very severe super thin eyebrows that add a slightly surprised but sinister expression to her face.

Mrs. Snow White is not the class's favorite teacher, unlike the pleasant Fairy Tale character, she is strict and very harsh with us. I know what you're thinking...yes she does sound a bit more like the evil queen, but trust me on appearance, she's way too pretty to be an evil queen.

My twenty-first glance at the clock reveals two minutes to go! Mrs. Snow White seems to have that ability that only certain special teachers have, the ability to make time stand still. Suddenly my ears are alerted to a strange sound, the sound of silence. I can't hear any sounds in our classroom at all. Not Mrs. Snow White's voice, not the whispering of the two boys behind me, not even the scratching of Gretel's pencil (my best friend who is sitting next to me as she frantically takes notes as always). Not even the ticking of the wall clock I spent so much time staring at. I glance around the room, no noise, no talking, no movement, nothing! Mrs. Snow White has finally done it, she has actually made time stop altogether. Everyone, everything, is frozen in time! Except me, it must be my incredible skill to NOT listen that has let me escape the amazing powers of Mrs. Snow White.

I stand up and start to cautiously move around the room staring at my frozen classmates. I stop in front of Mr. Tall Dark and Handsome, real name Richard, I wave my hands in front of his face - no reaction, not even a blink.

Just as well, it probably would have been so embarrassing if he wasn't really frozen still.

Time to have some fun, sitting next to Mr. TDH is Linda Douglas. Linda seems determined to come between me and Mr. Tall Dark and Handsome and has ruthlessly pursued him. I grab Linda's hand and move it up towards her face. I straighten out one of her fingers and push it up her nose as far as it will go. I step back to admire my handy work with a laugh...when an idea springs to mind. I race back to my desk, peeled off a pea-sized piece of dried glue from my glue stick and use a pen to color it green. I rush back to Linda and remove the finger from her nose and carefully place the green-colored glue on the tip of her nostril. The glue sticks nicely. This should be a good look when time starts up again.

Next, I move to Peter Kirk, the meanest bully in the class. On the way, I gently remove the lovely pink bow Melody likes to wear in her hair and carefully transfer it into Ted's unruly spikey hair

Finally, I move to Mrs. Snow White who is sitting behind the teacher's desk at the front of the room. I stand back and consider my options. I spot a very thick marker pen on her desk. I quickly grab the pen and remove the lid. I use my best art skills to quickly do one very thick red eyebrow over

Mrs. Snow White's severe thin one. I finish and step back to admire an eyebrow that any clown would be proud of.

My work is done and in fear that time may restart at any moment, I hurriedly return to my desk. I sit and stare at the clock, smiling at the thought of what will happen when my tricks are revealed. Gradually I grow tired and feel my head drift towards the desk. I'm aware of the thump of my head on the desk, fractionally ahead of hearing the sound of the lunch bell.

As I lift my dazed head, I realize two things. I must have fallen asleep and that I can hear many of my classmates laughing. I open my eyes with the expectation of seeing the laughing children staring at Linda, Peter and Mrs. Snow White.

In horror, I realize they are staring and laughing at me! Mrs. Snow White with her thin and normal colored eyebrows raised, asks if I have finished my little rest. Linda standing next to Mr. TDH with no pretend snot on her nose and Peter with no pink ribbon in his hair. Oh no, it was all a dream!

Most of the lunchtime involves me dealing with my classmates and their funny comments about me falling asleep in class. This may take a long time to live down. The rest of the day passes quickly and I happily escape school to rush home.

Home! My mom, whom I call Mrs. Absolutely Positive, greets me as I enter the lounge room. "I bet you had a marvelous day at school, another fulfilling step on your life of learning," she gushes. Now you know where her nickname came from! She means well but her constant positiveness sometimes collides with my reality of being an almost cool girl.

My dad who has a voice so loud I've nicknamed him Mr. Boom Boom is on his way home. Mom says when he gets home we're all going to pick up a surprise dad has organized. Dad's previous surprises have included me joining a soccer team and doing a two-day circus trapeze course. So you can understand why I feel a little nervous.

Dad arrives home and soon all three of us are back on the road heading off somewhere. Mom and dad are all smiles and happiness and from the conversations it seems that I'm the only one in the dark about the surprise.

We finally arrive at the front gate of what appears to be a small farm. Dad jumps out and opens the gate and Mom drives through with Dad reclosing the gate after us. We then bump down a little dirt track until we reach a small farmhouse.

Dad ushers us up to the front door where we are met by a really old lady.

I hear those magic words every child loves to hear, "You must be the puppy's new family?" I pretty much didn't hear anything else after that. The lady let us out to her backyard with the cutest little puppy I had ever seen stood wagging a tiny little tail. It waddles over to me and when I reach down towards it the puppy rolls over onto it's back and presents his tummy to me for a tummy rub. "It looks like Buddy and you will be great friends", said the lady. "Boston Terrior's have such lovely natures."

I gaze up at my parents with the puppy now sitting at my feet. "Is he really ours?" I ask.

Both my parents smile and Dad replies in what is a whisper to him, so as not to scare the puppy, "Yes Maddi, we thought a new puppy would be good for all of us, and a *buddy* for our Great Dane Tyson."

During the trip home Buddy is so super duper cute. He curls up and buries his head under my arm. Every now and again he raises his head and licks my hand wagging his cute little tail. I whisper into his little ear that we will be friends forever and I will always look after him.

When we arrived home, Buddy's first meeting with our giant black Great Dane Tyson was pretty funny. We put Buddy on the floor and Tyson walked over towards him, Buddy took one look at him and started making whimpering noises. Tyson just leaned over and started licking Buddy with his big slobbery tongue. After about the third lick Buddy's little tail started wagging and by the fifth, Buddy was jumping up on Tyson's face and licking him back. I could see they were going to be great friends.

Friday Night

Mom let Buddy sleep in my room as it's his first night with us. After tonight his bedroom will be the laundry as he needs to have his own place to sleep and it has a tiled floor. I didn't argue, I am just happy to have Buddy in my room for tonight.

I am way too excited to sleep...at first preferring to play with Buddy. Unfortunately, he keeps falling asleep but I stay awake for hours just staring at him. Eventually, I fell asleep on the floor next to him. The newspapers mom made me spread on the floor are a bit annoying, they rustled every time I move. I wake to a cold wet nose pressed into my face with a loud sniffing noise. So tired! I crawl back onto my bed and try to go to sleep. But I am now wide-awake! He keeps running around playing with his squeaky toy and jumping up onto the side of the bed trying to pull himself up to me. I give in, even though I know he's not supposed to be on the bed, and pull him up.

No sleep for Maddi. After about an hour...the Buddy battery goes flat and he falls asleep lying on my feet. At last, a chance to sleep, but I couldn't fall back to sleep with him on my feet. So very, very slowly I edge one foot out from underneath him. Buddy stirs but doesn't wake up. Now for the second foot, slowly and carefully as his head is balanced on it. I almost have it out when those beautiful puppy eyes snap open, the tail starts wagging and I endure another 20 minutes of play. Finally, Buddy is totally exhausted and collapses on my face. This isn't going to work! So I gently pick him up and put him on his soft and fluffy bed on the floor. Ahhh...sleep time.

I fall into a deep sleep, only to wake up a short time later, as Buddy licks my hand that is hanging over the side of my bed. Playtime starts again until finally I fall into such a deep sleep I am no longer aware if Buddy was awake or asleep.

When next I finally open my eyes it is daylight. I stay as still as a store dummy, hoping that Buddy is still asleep and trying to drift back to sleep. Then my nose detects a rather unpleasant odor, definitely a poo smell. Buddy was still sleeping on his bed but had left three lots of tiny puppy poos around the room. Good news...bad news. Two of the piles of poo were on the newspaper, yay! One missed the newspaper and is on the wooden floor, not so yay!

I creep out of my room to tell Mom of the poo emergency. She is very unsympathetic. She lectures, "Well Madonna (as soon as she called me Madonna I knew this was going to end badly), part of being a responsible pet owner is not just playing with your dog but feeding and cleaning up after him. So you know where the cleaning stuff is, best you get busy."

The bits on the paper are easy, I just roll up the paper, poo and all and drop them into a bag and then tie up the ends. It wasn't too hard to hold my breath that long.

The one on the wooden floorboards is not so easy and quick. Gingerly I open a bag and try to scoop it up in one go. Think I deserve a C minus for poo scooping, I get some poo on the top of the bag. Have you ever tried to tie up a plastic bag with poo on the top ends? Believe me, it's not easy and I got poo all over my fingers. Brainwave! I grab a second bag and drop the first bag inside it and quickly tie it. However, a large amount of poo stays on the floor, in fact, it is now smeared all over the floor. YUCK! I run off to get paper towels from the kitchen to wipe it up.

Disaster! Buddy has woken up...just what I needed! And he is running around the room with one of his toys. Sounds cute, but only if you didn't notice that he had run through the poo still on the floor and spread it around many other places on the floor.

Then one of those please freeze the time moments came along. Buddy was looking at my bed, his ears were pointing backwards and I could read his mind. He was going to jump on my bed! He had poo on his paws. A disaster was about to happen...and then he jumped. My cream colored fluffy blanket was covered with brown icky-sticky poo! I felt like vomiting! It was disgusting!

The cleaning job is spiraling out of control. I take buddy outside and hose him off and dry his feet. Leaving Buddy or Mr. Mess (as I'm thinking of changing his name to) outside. I sneak my blanket outside and hose it off too, then I tiptoe to the laundry and put it in the washing machine. Finally, I head back to my room and scrub off any remaining poo and mop the entire floor. Lucky for Buddy that I love him!

Monday

I don't really want to go to school today. I'd much rather stay home and play with Buddy. This is the second week with our new Principal, Mrs. Cook. Our old Principal Mr. Hi-5 had decided to retire. As you can tell from his name Mr. Hi-5 was a pretty nice Principal, he knew all the kids by name and used to walk around High-fiving kids at lunchtime. I don't think he did anything else, but at least he was nice to the kids.

Mrs. Cook has only appeared in public once in the two weeks since she has taken over as the school Principal. She came to assembly once and briefly went mad at the whole school because there was some litter on the edge of the oval.

She is a medium height, older lady (probably about 100...okay, maybe 70) with very short iron-grey hair and a pair of glasses with a colorful frame that the English singer, Elton John, would be proud of. Obviously, a nickname for her was no challenge. Granny sprang to mind immediately. But not like a kindly granny in the TV shows...more like the sinister mean granny in those scary movies.

The second time she was spotted outside her office was when she once again suddenly showed up on parade. Our Deputy Principal, Mrs. She Who Runs the school, was actually in the middle of handing out Student Awards. I thought, *that's nice, Mrs. Cook must want to meet the students who won the Student of the Week Awards in perso...* wrong! As my class is at the front of the assembly, we can hear the whispered conversation between Mrs. Cook and her Deputy Principal. Mrs. Cook first snatches the microphone out of the Deputy's hand then quietly but harshly says, "You are letting the assembly make way too much noise! I can't work in my office with all this noise."

18

Mrs. She Who Runs the School looks confused, then annoyed. She replies just as curtly, "Mrs. Cook they are just clapping the students of the week as they receive their certificates."

Mrs. Cook put a little more ice in her voice and instructs the Deputy to give out the rest of the certificates quickly, but to instruct the children to hold the applause and let them give one short clap at the end for all the certificate winners. With that she drops the microphone onto the ground, which sent a sonic boom through the speakers...then she storms off with the clacking of her high heels.

The Deputy Principal lets out a sigh, bends down and picks up the microphone. Following Mrs. Cook instructions she quickly finishes the parade.

So Gretel and I walk around the corner heading towards our PE lesson in the hall after changing into our sports clothes. We literally bump into Mrs. Cook who is rushing around the corner in the opposite direction. Gretel and I came out with "sorry" at the same time as Mrs. Cook snaps, "Why aren't you girls in class?" Before we can even reply she continues, "Those aren't your correct uniforms! Report to the office for a detention at lunchtime." She's struts off with her high heels clacking without a backward glance.

Gretel and I hurry off to the PE lesson upset for getting in trouble. We explain to Mr. Grant why we were late and how we got in trouble just for being in our gym gear. He gets that *look* on his face that all teachers get when they don't agree with something another teacher did or said...but don't want to say anything. You know the same look that your mom or dad gets when they don't agree with what the other one has said you can or can't do. Mr. Grant shakes his head and says, "Don't worry girls, I'll talk to Mrs. Cook and sort this out."

Mr. Grant hopson the phone and after about a 10-minute conversation that featured about 50 *buts* from him, he hangs up. He sighs, then with a smile says, "Your detention is canceled, girls." We were very relieved and very grateful towards Mr. Grant...he is such a cool teacher!

Thankfully the rest of the day passes smoothly and I rush home to spend some time with Buddy. I burst through the front door and call out his name...but Mom shushes me and points to Buddy's bed. The sweet little thing is curled up and sound asleep.

Later that night, I regret letting him stay asleep. When Mom arranged the laundry for Buddy to sleep in, I didn't argue, no way I could survive another sleepless night like last night.

Did I mention my bedroom is quite close to the laundry? Yes, very close! In fact, close enough that I can hear Buddy scratching at the laundry door clearly. So close that when Buddy's scratching on the doorway didn't work I could hear the whimpering and howling so clearly that he could have been in the same room. I try ignoring it, I try my fingers in my ears, I try holding my pillow over my head...but nothing works. Three times I go to the laundry and pat him until he fell asleep, each time I have to be a ninja and creep soundlessly from the room.

Eventually, I fall into such a deep sleep that I wouldn't have heard a jet taking off in the house, let alone Buddy's demands for company. I still feel tired, but not as bad as the previous morning.

I creep out to the laundry, which is strangely quiet. Slowly, I opened the door and peep inside. All occupants of the laundry were fast asleep, yes that's right - I said all occupants. Little Buddy is sleeping peacefully in his comfortable bed while Mom and Dad sleep leaning against each other sprawled on the hard tile floor. Obviously now was not a good time to say good morning so I creep back out, have my breakfast and head off to school.

Wednesday

Mrs. Cook ruined my day today, something I feel she may make a habit of doing. Today she announced in the school newsletter that it was compulsory for all students to compete in the school swimming carnival on Friday. For the carnival, the school is divided into different sports houses and all the kids compete against each other scoring points in all the events to decide the Champion sports house. I'm in the blue house, called the sharks.

Normally, that would be no major problem. I would make sure that mom didn't get the newsletter and develop a terrible mystery illness that unfortunately would keep me home from school on Friday. However, her second announcement destroyed that plan quickly...she was pleased that from now on a copy of the newsletter would now be emailed directly to all parents to ensure no parent missed out on vital school information. In other words, in case some students made sure that the paper newsletter never made it home!

I can swim...but I'm no Olympic swimmer and the idea of floundering around in the pool while Mr. TDH looks on is not my idea of fun.

A brilliant idea strikes me! Perhaps I can get into mom's email account and delete the newsletter. All hope is not lost yet. On arrival at home, I immediately sense that my plan is doomed. Lying on the table is a pack of bright blue-colored paper, some cardboard toilet rolls, masking tape, blue body paint and scariest of all - a can of blue hair-coloring spray. Mom had obviously seen the email version of the school newsletter already. Drats!

My mom is great, please don't think me ungrateful, but she can get a little bit carried away sometimes. Yes, when Mrs. Absolutely Positive gets an idea she can get way too excited...verified by her next statement, "So Maddi, I read about the swimming carnival and I've grabbed a few items. You may not be the best swimmer but when I finish with you, you'll certainly look like the best supporter."

The afternoon is spent making pom-poms and mom experimenting with her artwork on my face, arms and legs. She was super keen to cover me in blue body pain, but I drew the line with that and the blue colored hair spray…as I had memories of how hard it was to wash out from another time when Mom dressed me up as a frog for a dress-up-day at school.

As a good daughter, I let Mom have her fun, I even use the pom-poms as I did my house war cry. Mom loves it, but there's no way I'll ever be doing that in public. My voice is so out of tune and my dance moves with the pom poms are just plain dangerous. I look and sound so bad that both Buddy and Tyson run off out of the house and both of them lay in the far corner of our yard with their paws covering their ears.

Luckily, after a hot bath and a bit of vigorous scrubbing, I'm transformed from a 'mom's gone mad with the blue drawings on my arms and face girl' back into ordinary old Maddi.

Friday

Mom wakes me at 6, an hour earlier than usual to get me made up for the swimming carnival. By the time Mom has finished with me I am blue from my hair to the Blue Socks on my feet. This is much worse than when we had a practice. Mom has gone totally over the top!

Dad comes in and announcers how amazing I look, I just think I look like an extra from that Avatar movie. My hair is thickly coated with blue spray and pulled back into a ponytail. If it feels thick and stiff and just yuck, my skin which is covered with blue body paint (I couldn't stop her) feels itchy and irritated. It is going to be a long, long day.

Mom is so proud of her handiwork she insists on taking me to school. Proudly she walks with me to my classroom. I don't see anyone else with colored skin or colored hair. Most people have a house colored shirt on. Some girls have a matching ribbon in their hair and some of the kids have a colored armband. I start to get a very bad feeling!

Mom whispers to me, "So many of your classmates have no team spirit."

A moment later we arrive at my classroom door. Granny (Mrs. Cook) is standing just outside my classroom, her piercing steel colored eyes look me up and down. She frowns and turns towards mom, "Are you responsible for the way this child is dressed?" she asks in a *not at all friendly* tone.

Oblivious to Granny's obvious displeasure mom starts to gush on about how she certainly was responsible for my appearance. "It wasn't easy," she says and then she continues on about how she doesn't mind as she feels that it is important for parents to show their support for school events.

Granny frowns, "Come to my office now!" Mom looked at me with a puzzled expression as we followed Granny to her office. Once there, Granny quickly asks me for my name and then starts addressing mom as Mrs. Bull.

Mom puts out her hand and introduces herself, "So pleased to meet you, my name is Mary..." Granny cuts her off.

"Mrs. Bull," replies Granny.

"Yes, that's me and my first name is Mary." Mom continues, "And what is your first name?"

"Mrs. Cook," Granny replies, almost spitting the words ut.

"No first name?" asks mom, in a *not so pleasant* tone of voice.

"Not at school," replies Granny. "I believe that using the first names of my staff implies a lack of respect."

Mom just lets out an, "Oh..." in response to this.

Granny sits at her desk without inviting mom or me to sit. "Mrs. Bull I have gone to great lengths to ensure that all parents are aware of my new school policy on sports competitions at school. I sent out a newsletter in both electronic and hard copy," she explains in a sarcastic tone.

"Of course Mrs. Cook, I saw the email version, that's how I knew which day to prepare Maddi for the carnival."

Granny turns her computer screen around towards Mom and asks her to read the third paragraph under the swimming carnival out loud. Mom complies, in a voice that gets softer as she reads on, "Students may wear a house colored shirt and girls a ribbon in their hair and boys an armband. No student is to have colored body paint or hair color. Pom-poms are also banned as they make a mess."

"Oh! I'm sorry," Mom apologizes. "I must have missed that bit when I read about the carnival. Although I must admit that it seems a pity for the children to miss out on the full dress-up experience."

"Well that's the new rule, so I'm afraid your daughter will have to return home and remove all that blue from her hair and body," replied Granny.

Mom then asks, "So which parent committee meeting did you get this rule approved at Mrs. Cook because I go to all of them, and to be honest I can't remember that rule ever being discussed and approved?"

Granny stutters and stammers and finally blurts out, "I haven't actually had it approved by the parent committee yet but I'm confident it will be."

Mom smiles, "In that case, Madonna you had better head back to your class and get ready for the swimming carnival because as Mrs. Cook knows...any rule changes have to be approved by the parent committee before they become official rules. Isn't that right dear?" she asks Mrs. Cook.

Granny's mouth looks like she has just eaten a whole lemon, reluctantly she replies "Yes, that's right, you may go to the carnival."

Mom's positive power wins over Granny's grumpy power.

My happiness continues as I join the class heading off to the swimming pool. My cool status is running high, as I am the only one with colored body paint and hairspray. Gretel and Mr. Tall Dark and Handsome are super impressed. At that moment...forget...*almost cool*, I'm totally cool! Okay, some of the cool gloss disappears when I get carried away and try some cheerleading moves with my pom poms. And it slides even lower when I sing some of our team songs. But being the only fully blue colored team member still outweighs that.

***

However, as my turn to race draws closer...my nerves begin to grow. I'm not the best swimmer and I really didn't want to embarrass myself in front of Mr. TDH. Then Gretel gave me some great advice, I should try and get a fantastic start, then at least I could say I led the race for a little while. Suddenly, my race is called to the starting blocks. And as I stand on the blocks, the end wall looks a long, long way away.

More pressure, Linda Douglas is lined up next to me. My brain thunders - must beat Linda, must beat Linda...hush brain, I'm trying to concentrate on the start.

From the corner of my eye, I see the starter raise his arm with the starting pistol. My leg muscles tense and suddenly spring off the blocks. I soared through the air my body in a perfect dive position. What a start, what reflexes! Just before my arms glide into my first stroke, I hear the starter pistol, then a second crack from the pistol. Oh no! False start! My head surfaces above the water and I turned in my lane to swim back to the wall. Half the swimmers are still on the blocks while half are in the pool with me swimming back to the wall. They must have followed me in when I false-started.

As I swim back to the wall I notice the water in my lane is blue, I look over my shoulder and a stream of blue is following me. The area surrounding the pool is quiet, with no race to cheer everyone is sitting and watching...wondering what will happen next.

In the quiet, Linda's voice, who didn't false start with me, is incredibly loud and clear. "Look! Maddi peed in the pool, the water around her is turning blue!"

This creates a frenzy of girls kicking and splashing to escape the spreading blue colored water. I try to protest my innocence but I'm not heard above the noise of squealing swimmers and laughing spectators.

The teachers send us all back to our team areas. Gretel and Mr. TDH try to shelter me from the teasing and I remove my swimming goggles revealing blue circles around my eyes. Most of the blue hair spray has washed out of my hair.

All the teachers are meeting on the pool deck and I could see Granny throwing her arms around in an angry manner. Mr. Grant the PE teacher comes over to me and looks at my blue circled eyes and asked was that colored hairspray did I have in my hair. After I tell him that it was blue, he smiles and replies, "That's a relief."

He walks over to the other teachers and Granny. After a few minutes of discussion, Granny grabs the microphone and announces, "The pool will not have to be drained and the carnival will continue. Maddi Bull did not urinate in the pool, I repeat Maddi Bull did not urinate in the pool, the carnival will continue."

Earth, please open up and swallow me now!!!

The race is to be rerun, but happily for me I'm disqualified for starting before the starter's gun went off. At least I don't have to worry about turning the water blue again. I just try to blend in with the rest of the spectators which isn't really that easy when your skin is still bluish. Most of the blue pain that was protected by my goggles, wipes off onto my towel.

Finally, the day ends and I rush home. Mom greets me enthusiastically as always. So I skip the bit about being disqualified and suspected of urinating in the pool, I just tell her it was an exciting day. Then I rush off to the bathroom to start the transformation from an oversized Smurf back to myself.

Sunday

After the usual three hours of Sunday morning housework, the house looks spotless. For an alternate hippie style mother, mom can be very conventional when it comes to clean and tidy...especially my bedroom. I realize that despite how much I love little Buddy, he can be quite painful with the way he chews up everything in reach of his mouth. Who could believe a magazine could be ripped up into so many pieces by those small teeth. Did you know that to a puppy, a chair leg is edible and that tiny bits of dog saliva drenched wood are very difficult to vacuum up?

After we had finished, mom took me down to the mall for a milkshake. On the way we picked up Gretel and of course, Buddy came too.

While we go inside the milk bar, Buddy sits outside tied up to a signpost. I feel bad about him being left outside but we can see him through the shop window so I know he is safe. Every second person stops and pats him. Buddy loves all the attention and rolls on his back for a tummy rub.

We had nearly finished our drinks and Gretel said, "I'm definitely going to have to talk my mom into getting a puppy."

I replied, "Yes, a dog is such fun, you'd be such a great dog mommy!"

Gretel gave a slightly embarrassed smile, "I'm sure...but more importantly, have you seen how many cute boys have stopped to pat him? That dog is a boy magnet!" Even mom laughed at that one.

We collect Buddy and go for a little walk around the outside of the shops. Mom had suggested Buddy might need to go to the toilet and told us to take him over to the grass footpath, that idea goes out the window when I see who is walking towards us. A good day turns into a great day when we run into Mr. TDH and his mom who have been shopping. Mr. THD is very proud of his new shirt, he is even wearing it home with his old shirt in the shopping bag. I must admit it looks gorgeous, so clean and white.

While our moms talk, Mr. TDH fusses over Buddy as this was the first time he has met him. Buddy loves Mr. TDH and jumps up on him licking his hand and any other part of his body he could reach. The feeling was obviously mutual! He picks him up for a cuddle and Buddy licks Mr. TDH's face.

Gretel and I stand there smiling and suddenly Gretel asks Mr. TDH, "Why is your shirt so wet?" Mr. TDH quickly puts Buddy down and gazes in horror at his new shirt, which has a huge wet patch with yellow liquid dripping onto his pants.

"I don't know what it is," said Mr. TDH, "but it feels warm."
Suddenly it dawns on me, Buddy has weed on Mr. TDH in
his excitement. My face goes red as I apologize to Mr. TDH,
"I'm so sorry, it's from Buddy."
Realization hits Mr. TDH. He rips off his shirt and holds it
gingerly by two fingers outstretched from his body as far as

his arms can reach. That got both mothers' attention really fast. Gretel quickly explains what has happened, I was too busy apologizing still. Mr. TDH and his mom head home quickly to wash out his wet and smelly shirt while mom reprimands me for not taking Buddy to the grass footpath when she told me to.

Wednesday

Towards the end of semester, the school traditionally has a Gold Pass day. The Gold Pass day is intended to reward all the students who display good behavior during that semester. So basically, if you don't get any detentions you get to go on the Gold Pass day activity.

I've never missed one yet so when our class teacher mentions this semester's activity I'm very excited. The Gold Pass students will be going to Inflatable World, the newest water theme park in our area. From the pictures our teacher put up from Inflatable World's website, it's got giant inflatable slides, obstacle courses and floating jumping castles. I can't wait this is going to be so much fun!

I think Mr. TDH has finally forgiven me for the shirt incident, although I have been avoiding him since because I am so embarrassed. Anyway Gretel and I sat with him at lunch today and he raved about how wonderful Buddy was, so I think all is forgiven.

Today I also developed a new interest in Robotics, I signed up for the School Robotics' Team. Gretel thinks that I only joined because Mr. TDH does it...but of course that isn't true! I've watched several Star Wars movies and always like those two robot guys.

Mrs. Smith held the meeting about Robotics for the people that signed up and it actually sounded really cool. We will learn to program these little robots and send them through a course, there is even an inter-school competition.

Tonight I'm studying up on the program booklet that Mrs. Smith gave us, I'm determined to do really well. Once we have mastered the basics of programming the Robots, Mrs. Smith said we will be able to take the robots home to practice on them.

The fact that Linda is also doing Robotics drives my ambition to be the best programmer at our school!

Friday

I love Robotics!!!!

No seriously! I really do...programming them to go where you want and doing what you tell them to do, is actually really cool. Some kids would never join the Robotics Program because they think it's just full of nerdy kids. Well, it is kind of a nerd hangout...but the Nerdy kids have three things going for them: they're really smart, they're really nice and they've been really kind and helpful to Mr. TDH and me. Thanks to our new friends we are getting really good at programming. Although I must admit getting to work with Mr. TDH also makes Robotics very cool. Maybe one day I'll work at NASA, my office door will read Maddi Bull Programmer - Mars & Beyond.

Saturday

I organize to meet with Gretel at ten to take Buddy for a walk. We have decided to take him to the off-leash dog exercise park in town, it has a gate and is fully fenced so we can let Buddy have a run around. I walk Buddy over to Gretel's house, which is only two streets away. I do all the walking as Buddy decided after about 1 minute that he was too tired to walk anymore, so I carry him. That, of course, leads to lots of people commenting on who's getting the exercise. One lady said to me, "I can see who the boss is."

Once I get to Gretel's house I don't have to carry Buddy anymore, Gretel carries him instead. When we reach the Dog Park and take Buddy's lead off, he suddenly is full of energy and starts running around sniffing all over the park. I throw the ball I bought for Buddy to play with, he chases the ball frantically, but once he catches it, he won't let go of it. He brings it really close to us and then runs away when we try to grab the ball to throw it again for him.

After many minutes of frantically chasing, Gretel and I actually collide and end up lying down on the grass. Buddy just moves to the shade of a nearby tree and watches us warily while he chews on his ball.

The fun really starts when we decide it is time to go home. Buddy wouldn't come to us, he thought we were still playing the chasing game for the ball. Our calls to Buddy went from nice, "Come here sweetie," to a screaming, "come here NOW!" Our attempts to catch him gave much amusement to the other dog park users, some were yelling advice...none of which was proving to be successful.

Eventually, we manage to trap Buddy in a corner and pounce on the rapidly tiring puppy. We quickly get the lead on him but when we attempt to walk him home he collapses on his stomach and totally refuses to move. Gretel and I take turns carrying him home. We arrive back at my place hot, tired and really sweaty.

Buddy, however, is rejuvenated and finds a squeaky toy and drops it at our feet. Hopefully, he looks at us with his big puppy eyes.

We both just groan and collapse onto the couch.

Sunday

Mom wakes me up, with her Mrs. Absolutely Positive loud voice and smile firmly fixed in place. "Let's take Buddy to the markets with us this morning," she says.

I sleepily drag myself out of bed and set about getting ready to go. It's then that I discover my favorite sandal or should I say…the many pieces of my favorite sandal. Tiny puppy bite-sized bits of my sandal are scattered about the floor of my room.

Mom's response to my complaining about Buddy destroying my shoe is, "Well you shouldn't have left your shoe lying on the floor," followed by the responsible pet owner lecture. Not the sympathy I was looking for.

Dad decides to join us and bring Tyson along as well. The five of us head off to the markets held at the football fields. Normally I'm not a keen market fan but these markets are kind of cool with lots of yummy food stalls and interesting stuff.

At the start, mom holds Buddy on his lead, and of course, Buddy is amazingly well behaved and cooperative. Buddy is the ultimate flirt! If a person looks at him his tail goes into hyper-drive and he gives out little whining noises. If they stop or talk to him he drops down, rolls over onto his back and hopes for a tummy rub. Tyson, as usual, is well behaved and I can see by the look on his proud face that he thinks Buddy is being a total pain. Every time Buddy tries to draw attention to himself, Tyson turns his head, looks at us and sighs.

As Gretel had noticed on an earlier outing Buddy is particularly really liked by young cute boys and he likes them back just as much. It's embarrassing because with each of the cute boys mom not only engages them in conversation but then proceeds to introduce me to them. How can that be bad you ask...because each time she introduces me she includes some interesting fact about me, one that isn't even true most times. For example, "What's your name? Josh, wow what a lovely name. You look very fit, this is my daughter Maddi she loves playing sport."

My list of incredible skills and abilities according to Mom include dancing, singing, snowboarding, gymnastics and probably going to the Olympics. When I complain to mom that she is embarrassing me she just laughs and assures me it is a parent's job to embarrass their child.

Mom then sends me off to get us some food with Buddy while she looks through some of the art stores.

I take Buddy's lead and head off, for the first few minutes Buddy co-operates well. Then he starts trying to go in the opposite direction back to Mom. When that doesn't work he promptly lays down. I spent several minutes trying to coax him to get up and follow me. Fail! He just lays there with his little tail wagging slowly.

Suddenly he leaps up and the tail starts wagging faster. Yay, I think, at last. He bolts straight past me over to a group of young boys...not just any boys, but a group that has at least three of the boys Mom had talked to earlier.

"Hey," goes one of the boys, "it's Maddi and Buddy. She's a dancer you know."

"No Clint, she's a snowboarder," said another boy.

A third boy adds in, "I thought she was a gymnast."

"I guess I'm just multi-skilled," I stammer, not really sure what to say, as my face goes bright red.

"Sorry got to go," I said as I scoop up Buddy and rush off into the crowd.

I join a long line in front of a stall selling Mexican food. I notice the people right behind me were Mr. Skeil, a teacher from school and his wife and small son who must be about four-years-old. We exchange an awkward hello. You know, the type when students and teachers meet outside of school...dreadfully embarrassing.

The line slowly shuffles forward, the smell of the food is making me hungry. Suddenly Mr. Skiel's son starts whimpering, the whimpering slowly grows louder until it is full on crying.

I politely ignore it, as I don't want to embarrass the teacher over his inability to control his child's behavior.

Then an angry voice snaps over the crying, "Look what your dog has done!"

I look down to see the little boy's ice cream cone is on the ground and Buddy's face is covered in strawberry ice cream.

I pull Buddy away from the little boy and start to apologize. Mr. Skiel declines my offer to pay for another ice cream but gives me a version of the *being a responsible pet owner speech* focusing on keeping your dog under control.

I'm too embarrassed to rejoin the line and instead hurry back to Mom. I explain what happened. She bursts into loud laughter, which embarrasses me even more. Finally she is able to control her herself and then agrees to find Dad and take us all home.

Monday

Monday starts out as a pretty normal Monday, although there was one awkward moment when I came face to face with Mr. Skiel in the hallway. However, he gave me a cheery, "Morning Maddi". Followed by, "How's your cute little pup going?" So lucky for me there are no hard feelings there!

On assembly today, Mrs. Cook spoke about the Gold Pass day, but not in a good way. Basically she explained that in her opinion the satisfaction of knowing you have done the right thing is all the reward you should need for displaying good behavior. She went on about how she thinks the Gold Pass idea is unnecessary and an unneeded expense for the school.

She followed up by saying, "However as the school has already committed to this concept before I assumed command of this school, I will allow this wasteful day to go ahead. There will be some very important changes to the allocation of attendance at this Gold Pass day. As of this moment to my amazement the entire student body has no recorded detentions, which I consider quite unbelievable and perhaps reflects on the staff failing to enforce our school rules effectively. I remember giving out two uniform detentions when I first arrived, but for some reason they are no longer recorded. And fortunately for the culprits, I can't remember who you are. So to my teachers, I say step up to the detention challenge and to my students,I say watch out."

The teachers around the assembly area don't look very happy with that comment and some low murmurs can be heard from them. She continues on with, "So any student breaking any rule between now and Gold Pass day will not be allowed to attend. Also, I will personally be patrolling during the school day to pick up any wrong doing that your teachers might have missed!"

With that she dismissed the assembly and stomped off to her office. I'm not sure who looked the most upset as we left the assembly…the kids or the teachers.

I'm feeling pretty excited today because my whole afternoon at school is devoted to the Robotics' group.
Miss Smith puts Mr. TDH and me with a kid called Charlie. Charlie is really nice and patient with us and we learned lots from him. Today we have been learning how to program the robot to go round a shape, like a square or rectangle or circle. We have a felt mat on the floor with the different shapes on it and we try to program the robot to follow around. The rectangle and square shapes are easier because they are basically straight lines with a 90-degree turn.

Mrs. Smith throws down a bigger challenge. She lays a huge sheet of white paper down on the floor and we have to connect a thick marker pen to our robot. We are still working in the same groups and our group is given a red marker. We have to draw a circle and an arrow and Mrs. Smith gave Charlie an extra challenge of writing our two names, Richard and Maddi. I bravely volunteer to control the robot to draw the circle (secretly hoping to show off a bit for Mr. TDH) leaving Mr. TDH the arrow.

54

Each group is given a small marked out area of the sheet of white paper to work in. Mrs. Smith said it's fine if any of our tasks overlap as our area is quite small. We quickly knuckle down and start working out our programs.

Of course, Charlie is finished first and his robot quickly and perfectly writes our names one on top of the other. Next, I did my circle, Charlie had advises me to do two semi circles and join the top of each. Might have worked for him...but not for me! My weird circle shape surrounds the two names that Charlie had written. As Mr. TDH starts his arrow, I realize my circle actually looked more like a heart shape. Mr. TDH's arrow goes straight between our two names, the arrow crossing my heart-shaped circle diagonally. As Mr. TDH's robot moves off the paper...this is what we had in front of us.

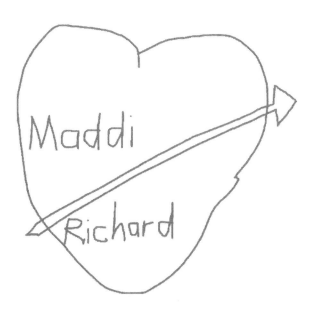

Both our faces blush bright red as Mrs. Smith gushes, "How romantic." That got everyone else's attention and they all burst into laughter, except for Linda Douglas who had a serious frown on her face.

Charlie looks at the paper and then back at us, "You guys are a lot better at Robotics than I realised," says Charlie in awe. I'm pretty sure my face stayed red the whole way home, but I do have to admit, it was kind of cute.

At Robotics, Mrs. Smith introduces us to new equipment we'll get to use at the Interschool Robotics Tournament. The new gear is amazing; each robot now has a little inbuilt camera which can be connected to a laptop so you can watch where it is going on the laptop screen. There is also a little antenna that also connects to the laptop so instructions to guide the robot's direction can be typed into the laptop and almost instantly relayed to the robot.

My mission to Mars seems closer every day. We have a great time using the new gear and of course...Charlie is the best. Mrs. Smith announces that the Robotics tournament will be held on Saturday at the local University. All our parents are invited and Mrs. Cook will also attend. Mrs. Smith then schedules several afternoon practices for us this week so we can get familiar with the new equipment.

Wednesday

With only two weeks to go until Gold Pass Day everyone is very nervous about getting busted for doing the wrong thing and missing out. Granny has made three unannounced visits to our class in the last two days bursting in through the door like she is some kind of one-woman swat team. She would always snap out the same thing, "Don't pay any attention to me! Just watch and listen to your teacher!"

Granny hasn't managed to catch any one in our room doing anything wrong but each time she wanders the room, she ends up standing behind me. Having her hovering just over my shoulder is very off-putting, especially when she would stay there for several minutes. When she finally leaves, you can hear the whole class, including the teacher, give a sigh of relief.

Saturday

The morning of the robotic tournament arrives and I wake up early. I had a very restless night's sleep. I'm feeling nervous about the tournament...worried I might mess up our team's chances. However, I'm probably more nervous about the fact that Mom and Dad are giving Mr. TDH and his mom a lift out to the University and we'll be arriving early, so the two moms will have plenty of time to talk.

I don't know about you...but when I get nervous I have to make lots of visits to the toilet. So by the time Mr. TDH and his mom arrive at our home, I've already made two quick trips to the toilet. Mom noticed and I had to assure her I was okay, just feeling nervous.

When our guests arrive dad is outside mowing the lawn, so it's just the four of us sitting in the living room. Of course, Buddy is sitting next to me on the chair, as always. Mr. TDH sits next to Buddy and gives him plenty of cuddles and we chat about the upcoming tournament.

At this stage, Tyson is starting to get a little jealous. Tyson decides to muscle in on the fun. He uses his nose to nudge Buddy off the chair and then climbs up on the couch with his head on my lap and his back half on Mr. TDH with his tail brushing against Mr. TDH's nose every time he wags it. Richard burst into laughter. "Your dogs are just like you, loveable and naughty at the same time."

Did he just say loveable or am I having another dream? I pinch myself to make sure this is really happening. Yep, it hurt, I'm awake!

I haven't told you yet, but Buddy has a very unpleasant habit of farting and you wouldn't believe how bad he smells. They are always silent but deadly. And they are even smellier than the Great Dane's.

So as luck would have it...just as I stood up to call Tyson off Richard, Buddy let out a very smelly one. I pretend not to notice and hope no one else smells it.

Just as the smell from the first one clears, a second erupts that's even worse than the first fart. About the same time, my own stomach starts to gurgle, oh no, I'm going to need to go to the toilet soon and everyone will think the earlier smells were from me.

Amazingly Buddy let's out a third fart. Mom says, "For goodness sakes Maddi, go to the toilet!"

Then to our guests she explains, "She's very nervous because of the tournament."

I feel the flush as my face goes bright red and start to say how it's not me, it's Buddy. However, at that moment, my own bowel decides this is all too much and I literally have to race to the toilet.

I finish my business but I am too embarrassed to leave the toilet. Finally, I hear dad yell out, "Hurry up Maddi! It's time to go."

I hurry out, wash my hands in the bathroom and race to the car where everyone else is already sitting. I'm in the back with Mr. TDH's mom sitting between Mr. TDH and myself.

Mr. TDH leans forward and winks. He whispers, "Lucky that Buddy isn't coming too, I don't think the air conditioning would cope."

I grin back, thank goodness Mr. TDH knows it wasn't me making the smells and this is his subtle way to let me know. He is so nice!

We arrive at the university and follow the signs to the Robotic Tournament rooms. There are lots of schools involved and heaps of kids heading along the pathways with us. We reach the entrance to the university building and Mrs. Smith is waiting there to sign in our school team and assign us our name tags.
Once that is done she instructs us to have a quick look around the tournament area and then to report to room C and the parents can take a seat in the tiered seating. The

tournament room is huge and has two levels the second level is up a short flight of steps.

Our parents head off to the seating area as Mr. TDH and I go to find room C. Dad sees this as a great opportunity to embarrass me and booms out a loud, "Go Maddi!" as we walk away from them. Mr. TDH laughs as I put my hand over my name badge and urge him to hurry up.

We find room C and already most of our team is in there. Mrs. Cook stands at the front of the room and snaps at us to sit down quickly. She keeps checking her watch every few minutes. Mrs. Smith soon walks in with the last few kids, and Mrs. Cook gives her watch a final long and angry glance. "Are they all here yet?" she demands of Mrs. Smith. Mrs. Smith smiles and nods.

Then Mrs. Cook launches into a speech...but not quite the speech we were expecting. Basically she emphasises how we are representing the school and how important winning is as it will add prestige to our school. According to her...we should give a one hundred percent effort to ensure our school wins and not let her down.

Mrs. Smith looks a little shocked by the tone of Mrs. Cook's speech.

Mrs. Smith announces, "Good luck students, Mrs. Cook and I will enjoy watching you participate in such an exciting day."

Mrs. Cook butts in, "Unfortunately I'm far too busy to stay and watch. Mrs. Smith, you can report to me on Monday morning." Then without another word she quickly leaves the room.

Mrs. Smith looks embarrassed, "You'll compete with your usual team partners and I've written the order of competition on these briefing sheets," she says.

She then continued, "Have fun, enjoy yourselves and make new friends. Winning isn't everything, I'm very proud of all of you."

Charlie, Mr. TDH and I are the last team listed to compete for our school. Our school area is on the upper level so we have a good view of not only our own competition table but also those tables below us. It's fun and exciting watching everyone else compete especially as it's a really supportive atmosphere. Everyone is clapping and cheering each round winner during the events, regardless of which school wins.

As we head into the final rounds three schools have been clearly dominant, Wolston Park, Greenfields Academy (an exclusive private school) and our school Harper Valley. In the middle of all the excitement I feel a small knot of anxiety starting to grow in my stomach. Inside my head I'm quietly hoping we don't end up with our team's performance deciding if our school wins or loses.

Of course that's what happens, going into the final round of competition, Wolston Park has fallen behind so only Greenfields Academy and Harper Valley can win.

As we prepare for our event, I can hear our teammates who are gathered on the other side of the table encouraging us. In amongst the cheers, I hear Linda Douglas say loudly, "At least they have Charlie and Richard." I try to ignore her but it breaks my concentration and I struggle to program my robot in the fifteen minutes allowed.

The final task is to program the robot to go through an obstacle course, it looks quite difficult. We can use the new equipment to adjust the robot's program as it passes through the course but the robot will stop during the reprogramming. So it's faster to get the programing right in the first place. The team with the fastest two finishers from their team of three will win the round and the whole tournament for their school.

The supervisors sound the start hooter and the final round is on. Charlie's robot flies through the course but he stops it just short of the finish line. He explains that as he hadn't crossed the finish line he can still send his robot back to help if one of our robots get stuck. A wise boy that Charlie, minutes later Mr. TDH's robot gets hooked up on the rail of a bridge halfway through the course.

Charlie calls out, "I'll send my robot back and push you off the bridge!"

"No!" I reply, "I'm closer, I'll push him free with my robot." I quickly start typing my programing changes into my laptop. My robot stops as I program in the changes. I finish, hit enter and my robot surges into life. It speeds through the course and reaches the bridge. It loses a bit of speed when entering the bridge but finally it reaches Mr. TDH's robot but only gives it a gentle nudge. Not only does Mr. TDH's robot not get knocked free…but my robot comes to a halt against Mr. TDH's robot.

I hit the keyboard again and my new programing sees my robot back-up and then accelerate towards Mr. TDH's robot at full speed. It slams into it with a thud, but Mr. TDH's Robot remains stuck. Frantically I key in new instructions and my robot backs up again but even further this time. Once again it accelerates towards Mr. TDH's robot.

This time it hits the other robot so hard it gets airborne. I watch in horror as my robot flies off the table over the railing that separates the top level from the bottom level and lands on the Greenfield's table. Not just on their table but actually on top of one of their robots. It bounces off the other robot, taking the communication antenna with it. My robot lands upside down, it's little wheels spinning uselessly.

The Greenfield Academy robot is obviously damaged and out of control, just spinning around and around in the same place. I race down the steps to retrieve my robot, the audience sits in stunned silence. Except for my Dad who booms out, "Way to go Madonna!"

Meanwhile, Charlie sends back his robot to Mr. TDH's robot and starts to push it towards the finish line. I'm still apologizing to the other school's team as I reach across the table to pick up my robot. My shirt sleeve gets caught on one of the still functioning Greenfield's robots just as my hand closes on my robot.

As I pull back my arm clutching my robot, the Greenfield robot snags on my arm and comes too. The robot's spinning wheels continue to run and it gets even more caught up in my shirt.

Now I've got two Greenfield's kids and a Greenfield's teacher frantically tugging at my shirt trying to untangle their robot's wheels from my shirt.

Above all the noise I hear the supervisor at our table announce, "Harper Valley have completed the task!"

The *we've won* thought briefly flashes through my head before my ears are assaulted by the protests of the Greenfield's team. "They cheated!" "She broke our robot and she stole our robot off our table!" are the most popular comments being yelled. I feel so embarrassed; I just want to disappear into the floor.

The two supervisors meet on the stairs between the two levels and engage in a whispered conversation. It appears that one of them is upset which is not a good sign.

By now the Greenfield's teacher has finally untangled her team's robot from my shirt and I slink back up the stairs to re-join my team. An excited Charlie and Mr. TDH both give me a hug. I realize then that they haven't seen the destruction I have caused below on the Greenfield's team.

The supervisors finish their conversation and the one from the Greenfield's table asks for everyone to be quiet. She then announces, "We have a winning team. As this is not robot wars (this is followed by a giggle from the audience), the Harper Valley team has interfered with the Greenfield's team's robots and is disqualified. I declare the Greenfield's team are the tournament champions."

The crowd claps enthusiastically, I quickly explain to Charlie and Richard what had happened at the Greenfield's table. The three of us then go and congratulate the winners.

Mrs. Smith comes over to us with a big smile and gives us all a hug, with a, "Well done team." She continues, "Without the bad luck you would have finished ahead of them, even if Maddi's robot hadn't landed on their table. But it's fair that we are disqualified. After all, Maddi did single handily take out two thirds of their team."

I think it's going to take a long time to live this one down. At least the car ride home was fun. We laughed all the way home with dad's entertaining description of what it looked like from the stands. Even I had to laugh when Dad referred to me as destructo daughter.

Wednesday

Costume ball, that's right ball...not dance, not disco, but a costume ball! Mrs. Cook continues on her mission to destroy the lives of all her students. This morning she announced that the school dance held at the end of each term would now become a costume ball instead.

We would all be taught how to "dance properly". We would learn the formal dances (old fashion dances) and no modern dancing would be allowed at all. Mr Grant and some volunteer helpers will teach the dances in our normal Sport lesson times.

That brings a groan from all the students who love sport, knowing Dodgeball would soon be replaced and the only ball in the school gym would be the ball in ballroom dancing.

Thursday

Our first dance lesson which is about to start, nervously our class herds together. Everyone tries to avoid standing at the front. Mr. Grant introduces the two volunteers standing beside him. The first is a lady with gray hair, Mrs. Velderham and an older gentleman who also has completely gray hair, named Mr. Steiner. Mr. Grant informs us that both helpers are good friends of Mrs. Cook and we should be grateful that they are giving their time to teach us.

I think Mr. Grant was letting us know they are Granny's friends so we don't say anything negative about ballroom dancing.

Mr. Grant tells us to grab a partner and form a circle on the floor. Nervously our class shuffles about, no-one is keen to make the first move to choose a partner. I start to edge towards Richard when Linda Douglas sweeps in out of nowhere and grabs him by the hand and drags him away. Suddenly, a flurry of partner grabbing occurs and before you know it I'm left standing with the only other partnerless boy, Peter Kirk. Mr. Grant yells, "Hurry up you two, join the circle, everyone is waiting for you."

We quickly shuffle into place and then Mr. Steiner informs all the couples that first we will be learning the Pride of Erin. He tells us it is a dance dating back to 1911 in Britain.

Gretel is just behind me and she whispers, "I think Mr. Steiner might have been there when they did the first dance."

I try to stifle a giggle but it escapes anyway and attracts the evil eyes of Mr. Steiner.

"You! Why do you laugh? Do you think history is funny? The trouble with you young people is that you have no respect for the past and your elders. Come here, you will be my dance partner as I demonstrate the dance," he snaps at me.

Thanks Gretel!!!

He then proceeds to try and demonstrate the dance with me desperately trying to following his instructions. I'm hopeless and just don't get it! But because I got in trouble for laughing earlier, at least no one else is going to laugh at me. Eventually he gives up on me and orders me back to my partner with a parting comment, "Try not to kill your partner."

Mr. Steiner then partners with Mrs. Velderham to properly demonstrate the dance.

It's very complicated with a lot of hand-holding and forward and backward steps and twirling. A recipe for disaster when dealing with twenty-six clumsy students. Both of them have this weird fixed smile on their faces. I wonder if it is a real smile or are they just pretending to like this dance or are they in pain?

Fortunately, I was not the first to trip anyone over, that honor went to Sally Pearson who stepped back when everyone else was going forward, tripping the girl behind her who went sprawling onto the floor.

You may have noted that I said *I wasn't the first to trip anyone over*...yes that's right, I am the second kid to bring someone down.

When I twirl away from my partner I tangle with Gretel and we both end up on the floor. Mr. Grant, perhaps worried by the mounting carnage, calls a halt to the dance session.

Saturday

Costume ball plus Mrs. Absolutely Positive equals potential public embarrassment for Maddi Bull.

Mom is being very enthusiastic about finding a costume for me for the ball. My feeble protests about simple, like a small plastic to tiara on my head to make me a princess, are swept aside as Mum scans the Internet for 'something more dynamic' for her darling daughter. Her words not mine.

Pictures flash before my eyes as Mom flicks from one costume to the next on her computer screen. Suddenly Mom stops on a robot costume, it's kind of cute and as Mom says it will go nicely with my latest talent - robotics. The costume is fairly simple, cardboard boxes, one for the head and one for the body.

Mom and I spend the rest of the day locating items to make the robot costume. It's actually fun! Mom and I painting, cutting and gluing all the bits together to create robot Maddi. By the end of the afternoon when I try the boxes on it's all coming together very nicely.

"It doesn't look that special now Maddi, but when we paint it silver and bottle top lids are glued as dials and buttons, then it will look amazing." I honestly believe that mom actually really thinks this.

I think it looks a bit clunky and cumbersome, but the advantage of that is that I'll be able to get out of those dances and stay safely on the sidelines thinking of witty conversations to charm Mr. TDH.

Mom puts her arms on my shoulders and looks me in the eyes. "On the night I'll tape some aluminium foil around your arms and legs to give you that authentic robot look. You are going to be the star of the ball...no boring princess costume for my daughter."

I smile.

Thursday

With only a week to go my friends and I are still on track to make Gold Pass Day. Apparently Granny's banned list is now up to thirty-two students, with the latest poor kid caught because his food wrapper blew away in the wind at lunchtime and Granny caught him running after it on the cement. She said he was breaking the rules in two ways, littering and running on cement. When he explained that the wind had blown the wrapper away and he was just running after it so he could put it in the bin, she dropped the littering infringement but he still got banned from Gold Pass Day for running on the concrete. So unfair!

In class this morning, I had a bit of a problem when my research folder seemed to have disappeared from my desk. The folder had weeks of work for a project that is due soon and it contained several sheets that Mrs. Tompkins had already checked and given me feedback on. Mrs. Tompkins asked me if I had my name on my folder and I told her my name was both on the folder and on all the sheets inside that I had previously handed in to her. She said, "Don't worry Maddi I'm sure it will turn up."

About half an hour later, Linda Douglas who was just returning from going to the toilet, races up to Mrs. Tompkins calling out, "Look what I found out on the walkway, Maddi's folder! She must have dropped it on the way into class."

"Well done Linda, I'm sure Maddi is very grateful you found it," replies Mrs. Tompkins.

I thank Linda when she hands it to me but my suspicions are raised as I'm certain I had left my folder in my desk yesterday. A quick peep in my folder seems to show less sheets in there than I remember, suddenly my suspicions hit code RED LEVEL.

I put up my hand and ask Mrs. Tompkins if I may go to the toilet. Once she grants permission I race outside fearing what I may see. As I go out the door I can hear the click clacking of Mrs. Cook's high heels approaching, I can't see her but she must be coming from around the corner. That's when I spot several research folder sized pieces of paper blowing along the ground. I quickly sprint to them and start snatching them off the ground. The sound of the approaching heels is much closer now, I grab the last sheet and turn to walk back into class.

Behind me I hear the voice of Mrs. Cooke, "Where are you going young lady?"

"Just back into class Mrs. Cook," I reply.

"Good, back to work, every minute counts!"

As I enter the room I see the sheets are mine, from my research folder, each with my name clearly written on the top. If Mrs. Cook had found these laying on the ground there would have been no Gold Pass Day for Maddi.

I can't prove it but I'm certain that Linda Douglas took my folder and then threw some of the sheets on the ground to try and get me into trouble.

When I walk in with the sheets she is looking at me but quickly puts her head down when she sees the sheets in my hand. Not nice Linda Douglas! I'll remember this.

Our second dance lesson starts the same way. First, we mill around trying to avoid being at the front. I slowly push through the crowd aiming towards Mr.TDH. Today he's going to be my partner! Mr. Grant stands in the middle of the floor flanked by Mr. Steiner and Mrs. Velderham, both of whom are wearing looks that say why we are wasting our skills here.

Mr. Grant calls out, "Grab a partner and form a circle quickly." I burst through the few remaining kids between Richard and myself. From the opposite side I can see Linda Douglas approaching just as rapidly. I dive for his hand and grab it spinning him away from Linda. Linda is moving too fast to stop and ploughs into Richard's back pushing him into me. I actually have to grab him to stop us both from falling over.

Smiling triumphantly, I lead Mr. TDH out to the circle on the floor. Suddenly as we stand waiting for the instructions, the audacity of what I had just done hit me. I felt a rush of heat that started at my face and seemed to spread to my entire body.

Mrs. Velderham explains that today we will be doing a progressive barn dance, which means that at a certain point of the dance, the girl's line would step forward and change to a new partner.

I can't believe it, all my effort to be Mr.TDH's partner will be for nothing. The music starts to play and Mr. Steiner calls out the dance instructions for us. As Mr. TDH takes my hand the nerves really hit me. I don't remember if I told you or not, but when I get really nervous...I sweat. I get really sweaty hands. So sweaty that I could probably solve the drought problems in the Sahara Desert.

So no surprise, I feel the little beads of sweat start to trickle down my arms from my hands. I hope my sweat isn't trickling down Mr. TDH's arm as well, that would be rather gross for him. That thought makes my hands sweat even more and now our hands pressing together are making squelching noises.

I'm sure Mr. TDH will never want to dance with me again. It's actually a relief when we get to the part when we change partners. I quickly wipe my hands on my shirt before I move on to my next partner.

The dancing goes on for what seems like forever. I'm slowly moving around the circle back towards Richard. I might get another turn with him yet. A few girls ahead of me I see Linda Douglas. She moves up to become his partner. She gives him a big smile and to my annoyance he returns it with a huge smile of his own. Just as we reach the part where the girl should move on the music stops.

Mr. Grant is talking but my attention is on Mr. TDH and Linda. Despite the dance having stopped she is still holding his hand! Finally, I hear Mr. Grant's voice telling us to line up and get ready to move back to class. It's only then that Linda releases his hand.

I feel my heart sink and numbly I line up. The empty space next to me in the line is suddenly filled by Mr. TDH. He starts to say something to me but I just turn and walk to the end of the line.

Friday

I arrive at school still in a grumpy mood from the Linda Douglas *hand-holding incident* yesterday. I'm talking to Gretel outside the classroom when Richard arrives and comes straight over to us. I restrict my replies to his attempts to make conversation to yes or no, then I drag Gretel away and go into class.

Gretel says, "You're being rude to Richard, it's not his fault if Linda didn't let go of his hand." Before we can continue this conversation, the teacher starts the lesson.

I notice Mr TDH casting glances my way a few times during the morning. I also note that he seems to be having very little interaction with Linda. Perhaps I have been a little bit unfair to the poor boy. So at lunchtime, when Richard asks if he can sit with Gretel and I, I respond with yes and a welcoming smile. I'm such a kind and wonderful person. He seems to be very relieved that the frosty atmosphere has evaporated and talks to me non-stop during the break.

Happy days are here again!

Wednesday Gold Pass Day

At last the day is here, my two best friends and I have all made it with perfect behavior records. It's a beautiful sunny day, perfect for a trip to Inflatable World. The trip on the bus is noisy and filled with excited kids. Everyone is hyped up for a day of fun. We burst through the admission gates once our teachers finish giving us the last minute instructions and the place and time to meet at the end of the day.

Like most of the kids we head straight to the giant inflatable slides, they're enormous! First you have to climb about three flights of stairs, then once you reach the top there are three slides that are super steep and end in a pool of water. I'm a bit scared climbing up the stairs because being an inflatable there is quite a bit of movement, they actually sway a bit and having an army of kids climbing them probably doesn't help. When we finally get to the top, Gretel, Mr. TDH and I wait until we can get three lanes so that we can race each other. Mr. TDH wins! Gretel is second and I'm last. It's so much fun and we have about another five races, only one of which I manage to win, before our legs tire and we have to rest.

Feeling recovered we head over to the inflatable jumping castles which are floating on a huge pool. We bounce around on them for ages having a great time. Some of the more adventurous kids are doing all kinds of flips off the jumping castles into the water. I'm very impressed when Mr. TDH starts to join in with the flippers. He is quite good and does some impressive back flips.

After watching for a while, Gretel and I decide to join in. Both of us are pretty hopeless but make some impressive splashes as we belly and back flop.

We notice the other kids starting to point at the very top of the jumping castle, precariously perched at the top is Linda Douglas. My initial reaction is she must be crazy to be all the way up there. However, something about the way she stands makes her look like she really knows what she is doing. Raising her arms like an Olympic diver, she stands poised on the edge. I hear Mr. TDH let out a quiet "wow". Then without any hesitation she dives off the edge and on the way to the water does a perfect somersault and lands with a perfect pencil dive with hardly a splash. Everyone claps and cheers, even Gretel and I, but Mr. TDH seems way too enthusiastic for my liking.

That leads us into lunch which is pretty quick affair as we don't want to be too weighed down with food. We head over to the inflatable obstacle courses which look fantastic, there are two matching courses which run side by side so that people can race each other. The courses are floating on another pool and have balance beams, slides, large balls you have to climb over or around, and tunnels you have to crawl through.

We join the long line with Richard and I on one side and Gretel lined up on the other side, so we can race each other. We watch as we are waiting and after seeing many people fall into the water and have to come back and line up at the end, we realize just how difficult the course is. It takes me three goes before I reach the end of the course, twice I fell on the balance beams and once trying to get around the ball. The idea of us three racing only happened the first go, after that we kept being in different places in the line and not able to be matched up against each other.

I end up behind Mr. TDH in the line again, after he waits for me after his turn. When I glance across to see who I'm going to end up matched against on the course I see that Mr. TDH is going to go up against Linda Douglas. Now that's a dilemma do I ask him to swap with me so I go against her and risk her beating me, or let him go against her and give them something to talk about later. I decide to back myself and ask Richard to swap with me so I can race against Linda, he looks surprised, but agrees.

Finally, Linda and I reach the front of the line and beeper that signals go sounds. I sprint off along the balance beam, lose my balance and start to totter on the edge but by some miracle don't fall. Now Linda on the other course is ahead of me. I go as fast as I can, leaping on the slide that is next. I risk a glance over at Linda on the next course and see I have caught up a bit. I dive into the tunnel and worm my way through it at top speed. The last thing I have to get past is the giant ball. Last time I managed to edge around the side of it. In a split second I make the decision that going around it will be too slow, so I launch myself at the top of it. I land on my stomach lying atop the ball, very graceful and elegant to watch I'm sure. A quick glance towards Linda reveals she is trying to carefully edge around the outside of the ball. I slide down the ball to land on the other side and run across the final balance beam. I glance across to the finish line on the other course but Linda is nowhere to be seen. A closer look shows her swimming across the pool. She didn't complete the course. I have beaten her.

What a way to finish a great day. I spend the bus trip home telling Gretel and Richard of my victory in some much detail they both fall asleep. Must have been all the exercise...couldn't have been my story telling.

Friday Night – The Last Night of School

Tonight is the ball night; the last night I'll see Richard for three weeks. He's going away with his parents on a cruise and he'll have no internet access so we will be out of contact for the whole time.

So I'm super keen to get dressed in my costume and to get to the dance. Mom asks, "While I finish the final bits of your costume ready can you do the dishes." I go to the kitchen and start to wash the dishes, but I don't get too many done before I start to daydream about tonight.

From a distant place...I hear Mom calling my name and I rush out of the kitchen, (I know, a bit over-dramatic). It takes a while to get dressed with Mom fussing over my costume but at last I'm dressed. I must say I do look outstandingly good. But unfortunately another fifteen minutes is spent taking photos, you know what Moms are like with special occasion photos.

So we have to have the photos of the robot, Dad with the robot, Mom with the robot, Buddy with the Robot, Tyson with the robot and the most time consuming of all, the camera set on timer to get Mom, Dad, Buddy, Tyson and the Robot.

Finally, we are done and head out to the car. The drive to the school for the ball is awkward. Oh no, not because of anything we said to each other but because my costume doesn't really suit the car seat or seat belt. After much manoeuvring and a little bit of pushing and squashing Dad fits me into the car.

We park and make our way to the school hall. At the entrance Granny is greeting parents as they arrive with their children. She seems to be attempting a friendly smile but it looks more like a zombie grimace. She looks me up and down as we enter the doorway. She obviously doesn't recognise me but when she looks at mom, a deep frown flits across her face.

"Mrs. Bull, an interesting choice of costume considering what happened at the robotics tournament," says Mrs. Cook.

Mom replies, "Not really when you consider how well the school team did to achieve second out of all those schools." With that we swept past her and enter the main part of the hall.

Mr. Grant and the Costume Ball committee have done a marvelous job of decorating the hall. Combined with all the kids wandering about in their costumes, it looks fantastic. Maybe Mrs. Cook's idea of a costume ball wasn't so bad after all.

My parents sit down on some of the chairs set up around the walls of the hall. Meanwhile, I mingle with the envious children admiring my costume, not really. I'm a good robot but there are some fantastic costumes on show tonight...from what I can see through the narrow slit cut in the box. I catch sight of Linda Douglas in a princess costume attracting a lot of attention, I begin to question the wisdom of being a robot.

Then the dance music starts and things deteriorate rapidly. Mrs. Cook uses the PA system to make an announcement. "Welcome to our first ever Costume Ball and thank you to everyone here for making such a wonderful effort with the costumes. I'm so happy to see so many supportive parents here today. I hope everyone enjoys the night and I am so proud to be the leader of this amazing school."

Tricked you!

That is what she should have said, instead she yelled into the microphone, "All students are to find a partner for the first dance, do it quietly and hurry up!"

I'm 12 and I could do a better job! I look over at my mother and she is smirking and shaking her head. Dad is laughing out loud! Oh how I wish I could laugh as well....

I start to move to the side to carry out my plan...my costume is too cumbersome to dance in. Mr. Grant suddenly appears in front of my limited vision. "Come on Maddi, Mrs. Cook said that all students have to participate in the dance," he states firmly.

"But Mr. Grant, I'm clumsy enough in normal clothes let alone dressed in cardboard boxes with a very limited view of the hall," I reply.

He brushes off my objections and tells me, "Maddi, go and find a partner, I saw a nice lego-man over there who would make a perfect partner for you."

I wander on to the dance floor and find lego-man, moving as awkwardly as me. We survive the first dance amazingly well, no one ends up on the floor and we only have a few minor collisions.

The next dance is not so successful. It's the progressive barn dance. The trouble is when we change partners my side vision is so restricted I have trouble seeing the boy, let alone the boy's hand which I'm meant to grab. The first few changes of partners are merely embarrassing, the last one is a disaster of epic proportions.

As I move onto Peter Kirk as my partner, I try to grab his hand but miss altogether. Panicking slightly, I take another more forceful swipe, miss his hand but definitely didn't miss his head. I feel my hand slam into his face and my little finger slide into his eye.

He yells out, "My eye!" and clutches both hands to his face. We both stop and the rest of the dancers pile into us. The dance line grinds to a halt and someone stops the music.

Above the noise of the kids and parents, the loud clear voice of Peter Kirk can be heard, "She got my eye, she hit me in the face and nearly tore out my eye!"

The surrounding noise drowns out my apologies so I try and
pat him on the shoulder but unfortunately with my stiff
arms I misjudge and hit him on the back of his head. By
now, Mr. Grant is on the scene and applies his usual calm
manner to settle things down. He has a look at Peter's eye
and pronounces it will be okay and leads Peter away to
apply some ice.

Mrs. Cook announces, "Quickly students to your places, the
dance must go on."

With no partner, I quietly escape to a corner vowing to myself that I won't dance again. Standing alone I watch the others dance. Mr. TDH certainly catches my eye dressed as a very dashing Robin Hood. I feel a pang of jealousy as I see Princess Linda Douglas move on to become his dance partner.

I have to admit, she looks beautiful as a princess. I feel slightly better when she moves on to the next boy but I notice she keeps looking back over her shoulder at Richard…my Mr. TDH!

Finally, that dance ends and I successfully remain hidden in the corner for the next three dances. Then Mrs. Cook makes us all parade around the hall in a single file so that everyone can see our costumes. Then she announces the boy and girl winners of the best costumes.

Of course, Mr. TDH and I are announced the winners and have to waltz around in the middle of all the other students to the thunderous applause of all the parents and teachers.

No, not really, only kidding, again! After all, this is a Maddi story...not a fairy-tale. Some other kids, much cooler than Mr. TDH and robot girl, won and got a voucher for an ice cream from the canteen.

Mrs. Cook picks up the microphone again. Everyone has the same reaction...I can see a lot of eye rolling. "Students, attention students, this will be the last dance. I'm sure you are as keen to go home as I am. So hurry up and find a partner."

Across the other side of the hall, I see Linda Douglas race over to Richard. They have a quick conversation and I see him shake his head. Leaving Linda standing there, he starts walking in my direction. As he gets closer, he gives me a big smile. Bowing towards me he asks, "May I have the pleasure of this dance Maddi?"

Of course, I answer, "Yes," and we join the circle on the floor.

Despite having Mr. TDH as my partner...my dancing is still no better. But it's fun dancing with him and I enjoy it despite my clumsiness. Finally, the dance ends and we stand facing each other awkwardly. I wish him a great holiday...just as I hear his parents calling for him to hurry up.

94

Richard pulls out a red envelope from his pocket, I can see my name written on it.

Nervously he stammers, "I got you a card, open it when you get home," and hands it to me. My arms are so restricted I can't reach far enough to put it in my pocket. Realising this, Mr. TDH takes it back and slips it into the ventilation slot that Dad had cut into the back of my head box. His parents call him again and he gives me a smile as he says, "See you later," and hurries off.

On the trip home my heart is racing at a million miles an hour. I wonder what Mr. TDH has written in the card. The drive seems to last forever but finally we arrive home. Once we go into the house I race off to my room to take off my costume and read his card.

Buddy follows me in and starts trying to rip the foil off my legs. My puppy helper slows me down but at last I'm transformed back to Maddi with my robot costume lying on the floor.

I've just picked up the box to get out the card when Mom storms into the room. "Get yourself into the kitchen young lady and finish the dishes I asked you to do before we went to the ball," she doesn't sound happy.

"Just a minute mom, I just need to do something first," I replied.

A stern, "Now!" and a pointed finger towards the kitchen are answer enough that my card will have to wait. I dump the box in my hand onto the floor and head off to the kitchen.

After four hours, actually it was only ten minutes but did seem a lot longer, the dishes are finally done. I race off to my room to read the card. As soon as I walk into my room, the devastation is obvious. Sitting amid the mess is Buddy still chewing on the only intact box. Scattered amongst the chewed up cardboard I can see wet and slobbery bits of red envelope, the envelope which contained the card from Mr. TDH.

I start gathering the bits of envelope and discover some of them still contain pieces of card. I stockpile them into two piles on my student desk, one pile for envelope and one pile for card. When I appear to have collected all the bits I start to try and re-assemble the card.

Matching up wet chewed-up pieces of card is harder than your average jigsaw puzzle. Slowly but surely the card starts to take shape. The front of the card is a write off; the picture seems to have been of flowers but the dog dribble has made the ink run so it's too hard to make out the picture. The inside is in slightly better condition and I can clearly read:

Dear Maddi, thanks for always making me laugh and being a great partner at robotics. Would you be

Be what? My brain races with possibilities, but the most popular choice with my brain cells, is *girlfriend*.

The bottom part of the card was missing. Frantically I burrow through the mess on the floor but find nothing more of the card. Mr. TDH is away for three weeks! Can I last that long not knowing what he was asking me?

Meanwhile Buddy, who is still chewing on cardboard while lying on the floor makes a strange burp noise. As I turn my attention to him, he stands up and makes a few heaving movements. Then a pile of vomit spews from his mouth onto the bedroom floor. Clearly sticking up in the middle of the vomit is a piece of red envelope. YUCK! Do I really want to put my hands in a pile of dog vomit?

While I consider my next course of action, Buddy, obviously
feeling better, starts to lick the edge of the vomit pile.
Realizing he is about to re-eat the mess...I grab him and put
him outside my room and close the door.

Do you know that dog vomit smells really bad? You
probably do, but I bet you didn't know it also feels really
horrible when it is all warm and slimy. Yes, I put my fingers
into the vomit searching for any other fragments of card and
envelope.

Don't go all squeamish on me, you know you would have
done it too.

The only bit I could find was the bit I initially saw sticking
out of the mess. I carefully open and flatten it out to discover
another fragment of card. This could be it, the message

revealed. I pull out the card only to discover the writing it once contained is now a totally unreadable mess of smudged ink.

Disaster! My room smells of dog vomit, my fingers are dripping with dog vomit and I can't find out what Mr. TDH wrote for three weeks.

AGGGGHHHHHHHHHHHHH!

Poor Maddi!

I hope you loved Almost Cool Girl 4!!!

Can you do me a HUGE favour and leave a review?

Thank you so much!

Bill

(BTW secretly I'm an almost cool Dad)

Some other books you may enjoy...

Not just for boys!!!

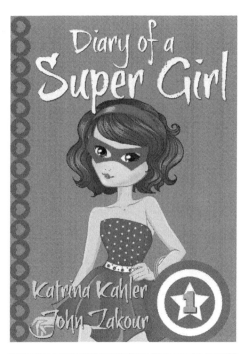

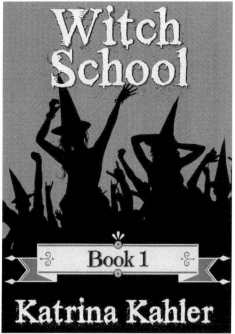

26962293R00059

Printed in Great Britain
by Amazon